Ollie's School Day

A YES-and-NO Book

by Stephanie Calmenson

illustrated by Abby Carter

Holiday House / New York

To Emily and Joshua—S. C.

For Carter and Samantha—A. C.

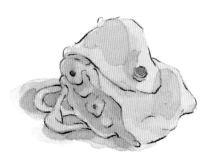

HOLIDAY HOUSE is registered in the U.S. Patent and Trademark Office.
Printed and Bound in September 2012 at Kwong Fat Offset Printing Co., Ltd.,
Dongguan City, China.
The text typeface is Alghera.
The artwork was created with watercolors.
www.holidayhouse.com

3 5 7 9 10 8 6 4 2

Library of Congress Cataloging-in-Publication Data
Calmenson, Stephanie.
Ollie's school day : a yes-and-no book / by Stephanie Calmenson ; illustrated by Abby Carter. — 1st ed.
p. cm.
Summary: Asks the reader a series of yes or no questions as Ollie gets dressed,
spends a day at school, and returns home.
ISBN 978-0-8234-2377-4 (hardcover)
[1. Schools—Fiction. 2. Day—Fiction. 3. Questions and answers.] I. Carter, Abby, ill. II. Title.
PZ7.C136Oll 2012
[E]—dc23
2011040357

Would you like to read an Ollie story?
YES?
Good! Let's get started.

It's a school day for Ollie.

"Please get dressed," says his mommy.
What will Ollie put on?

A bathing suit?

NO!

A space suit?

NO!

A police officer's uniform?

NO!

It's time for Ollie's breakfast.
"I'm hungry!" he says.
What will Ollie eat?

A bowl full of
bubblegum?

NO!

Fishy-flavor ice cream?

NO!

A sour pickle with mustard?

NO!

It's time for Ollie to go to school.
How will he get there?

Will he row a boat?
NO!

Will he ride a giraffe?
NO!

Will he hop to school backward?
NO!

Will Ollie
ride the bus
to school?

YES!

What will Ollie say when he sees his friends?

Will he say, "Good-bye!"?

NO!

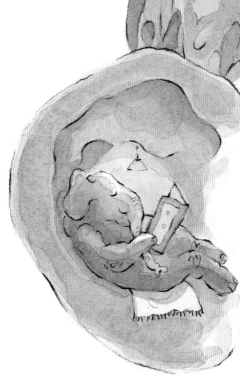

Will he say, "There's an elephant in my ear!"?

NO!

Will he say, "Woof! Woof!"?

NO!

Will Ollie say,
"Hi, let's play!"?

YES!

What will Ollie do when the teacher asks a question?

Will he jump up and do a backward flip? NO!

Will he drop his head on the table and start snoring? NO!

Will he sing "Three Blind Mice" as fast as he can? NO!

Will Ollie raise his hand and wait for the teacher to call on him?

YES!

It's snack time!
What will Ollie do?

Will he throw all the snacks to the squirrels?

NO!

Will he balance the snacks on his head?

NO!

Will he open a store and sell the snacks?

NO!

Will Ollie enjoy eating his snack with his friends?

YES!

What will Ollie do at story time?

Will he practice playing the kazoo?

NO!

Will he go for a swim in the sink?

NO!

Will he put on skates and zip around the room?

NO!

Will Ollie sit quietly and listen to his teacher read?

YES!

Is Ollie's teacher reading a funny book?

The Dog who Thought He was a Boy

YES!

When it's time for Ollie to go home, what will he do?

Will he jump up and do the hokey pokey? **NO!**

Will he say, "Good morning, teacher!"? NO!

Will he float up to the ceiling like a balloon? NO!

Will Ollie wave to his teacher and say,

"Bye! I had *fun* at school!"?

YES!

Who will be waiting for Ollie when he gets back home?

Will a whale be waiting? NO!

Will a juggler be waiting? NO!

Will a robot be waiting? NO!

Will someone who loves Ollie be waiting?

YES!

And he'll get a great big hug.